STOP THAT GARBAGE TRUCK!

Linda Glaser
Pictures by Karen Lee Schmidt

Albert Whitman & Company, Morton Grove, Illinois

To John and Laurel and Charlotte
with love and thanks. *L.G.*

For Dan Gheno. *K.L.S.*

Text © 1993 by Linda Glaser.
Illustrations © 1993 by Karen Lee Schmidt.
Published in 1993 by Albert Whitman & Company,
6340 Oakton Street, Morton Grove, Illinois 60053-2723.
Published simultaneously in Canada
by General Publishing, Limited, Toronto.
All rights reserved.
Design by Lucy Smith

Library of Congress Cataloging-in-Publication Data

Glaser, Linda.
Stop that garbage truck!/ Linda Glaser; illustrated by Karen Lee
Schmidt.

p. cm.

Summary: Shy Henry eagerly waits to see his "buddy" on
the garbage truck every time it comes— and finally manages
to speak on a day when there is a small emergency.
ISBN 0-8075-7626-3
[1. Refuse and refuse disposal— Fiction. 2. Bashfulness— Fiction.]
I. Schmidt, Karen Lee, ill. II. Title.
PZ7.G48047St 1993
[E]— dc20   92-22932
                                                       CIP
                                                        AC

It's early morning.
The streets are quiet and waiting.

Sylvie drives the empty garbage truck out to the street. Jackson and Frank swing on.

"Hey, Jackson," calls Frank. "We do Parker Street today."

"Good," says Jackson. "I'll see my buddy."

"That shy kid?" says Frank. "He won't even talk."

Jackson smiles. "He's still my buddy."

The truck rattles through the quiet, gray
streets. On Channing Way, the men jump off.
One-heave, two-heave, *crash*, *bang*, heave,
heave! Into the big white truck goes the
garbage!

A cat leaps off a lid. A dog barks from behind a gate. The men swing back on. And the truck rounds the corner onto Parker Street.

Henry opens his eyes. He listens and waits.
Is today the day? He listens harder.

Yes! Now he hears it— a deep, low thundering
and a long, high whine. *Rummble, rummble, eeee.*
Rummble, rummble, eeee.

He runs to the window. Cans full of garbage
line the sidewalks, waiting. Today *is* the day!

He pulls on his cowboy boots and gallops down the hall.

"Wake up!" Henry tugs Mommy's blankets. "The garbage truck is coming!"

Mommy's eyes squint open. "I know—I hear it." She closes her eyes.

Henry shakes the round hill of Mommy. "Get up!"

Mommy yawns. "Can't you watch it from the window today? I'm not even dressed!"

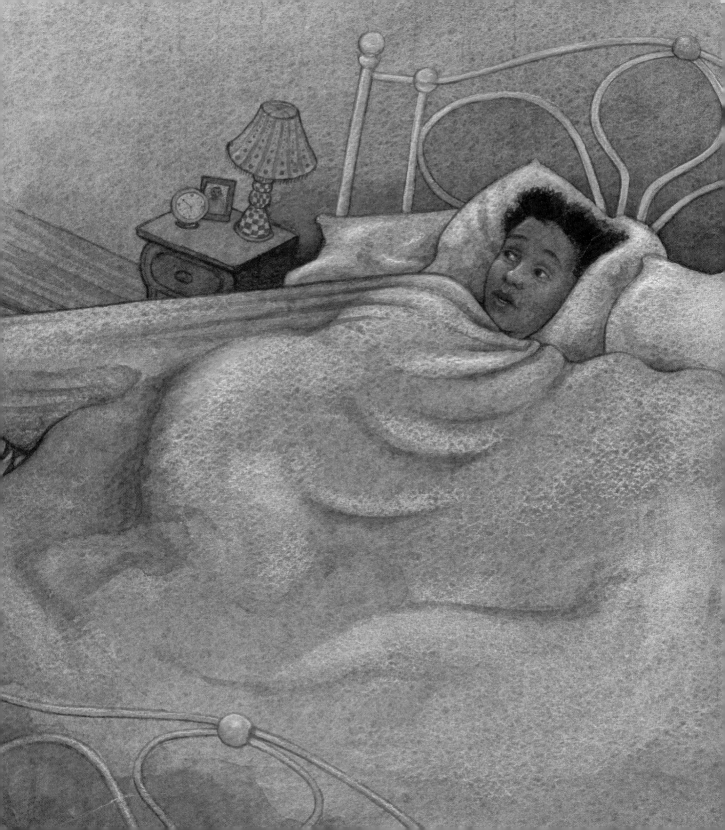

Rummble, rummble, eeee.

Henry runs to look. "Hurry, Mommy, it's coming! Hey, where's our garbage can?"

Mommy lifts her head. "Daddy took it out. Look again."

"Nope. It's not there."

Mommy springs to the window. "Oh, no! He must've forgotten!"

RUMMBLE, RUMMBLE, eeeee.

Mommy grabs her bathrobe. They race downstairs. Mommy unlocks the door. Henry swings it open.

Mommy dashes out back for the can. Henry runs out front. Hurry!

Here it comes!

RUMMBLE, RUMMBLE, eeee.
RUMMBLE, RUMMBLE, *eeeee.*
The truck stops right in front of Henry.
Yellow lights flash on and off. The huge mouth
opens like a hungry dragon's.

Jackson and Frank jump off. They lift the
neighbor's cans. One-heave, two-heave, *crash,
bang*, heave, heave!

"Hi buddy!" Jackson calls to Henry. "Are
you ready?"

Henry nods, just like always. Jackson tosses his cap high in the air. Ta-dah! He catches it neatly on his head.

Henry grins. Jackson laughs. "See you next week!" He jumps back on.

RUMMBLE, RUMMBLE, *eeee.*

Henry looks around. Mommy's not here yet! He wants to shout, "Stop! Wait for Mommy!" but the words won't come out.

Rummble, rummble, eeee—the truck rolls on.

Henry runs after it. He waves his arms.
The truck keeps going!

Henry runs harder. He takes a big breath.
"Hey!" he calls.
    Jackson turns. "What?"
    Henry fills his chest. "STOP!"

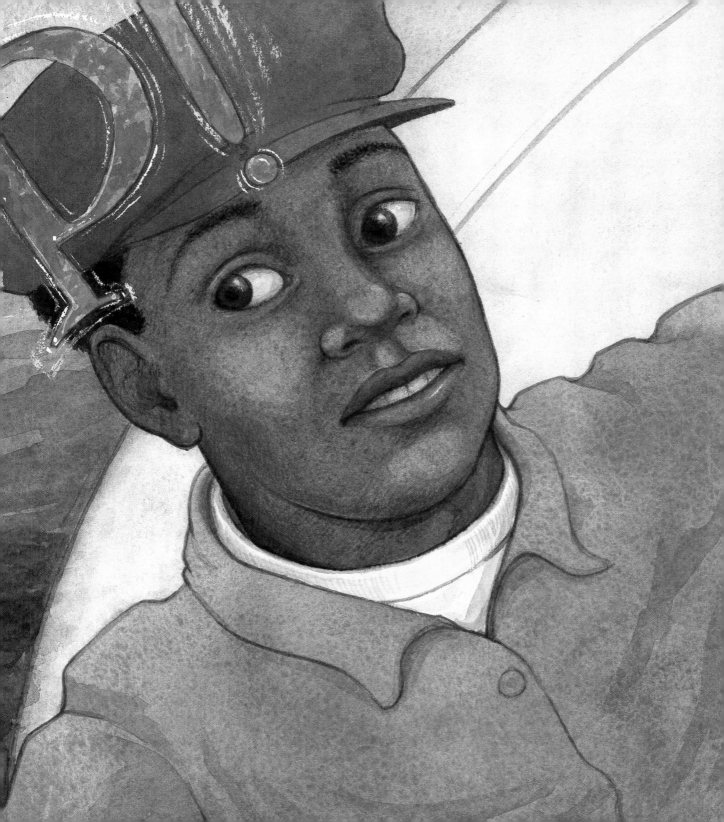

"HOLD IT, Sylvie!" Jackson yells.

Skreeee! The truck squeals to a halt.

Jackson grins at Frank. "My buddy here says STOP!"

Henry smiles. "You forgot our can."

Jackson looks. "We sure did. BACK UP!" he booms.

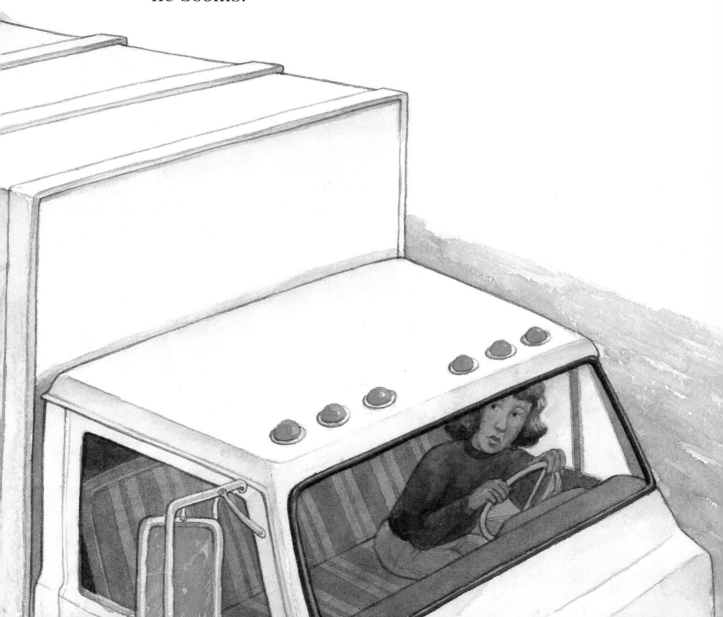

Beep-beep-beep. . .the truck rolls backwards.

Henry walks very tall. He leads it back to his house.

Now Mommy's out front, lugging the can.
"Thanks for waiting!" she gasps.

"Don't thank me—thank this fella." Jackson
winks at Henry.

Heave! Jackson swings their can high in the
air. Dump! Down into the dragon's mouth.

Crunch! The mighty jaws crush their garbage.

Honk. Honk. Sylvie taps the horn. "Let's go!" she calls. Jackson leaps back on.

The metal giant bellows. *Rummble, rummble, eeee. Rummble, rummble, eeee.*

Jackson sweeps off his cap. "Bye, buddy!"

Henry waves long and hard. "Goodbye!"
he calls. "Goodbye!"